The Weather Fairies

Dedicated to Liss Brothwell,
who is a little ray of sunshine

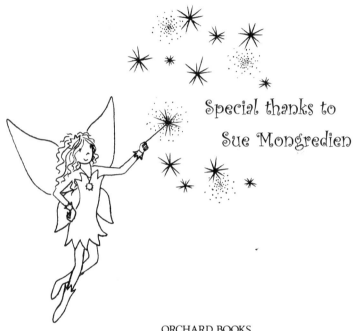

Special thanks to
Sue Mongredien

ORCHARD BOOKS
96 Leonard Street, London EC2A 4XD
Orchard Books Australia
32/45-51 Huntley Street, Alexandria, NSW 2015
A Paperback Original
First published in Great Britain in 2004
Rainbow Magic is a registered trademark of Working Partners Limited
Series created by Working Partners Limited, London W6 0QT
Text © Working Partners Limited 2004
Illustrations © Georgie Ripper 2004
The right of Georgie Ripper to be identified as the illustrator
of this work has been asserted by her in accordance
with the Copyright, Designs and Patents Act, 1988.
A CIP catalogue record for this book is available
from the British Library.
ISBN 1 84362 641 1
10
Printed in China

Goldie
the Sunshine
Fairy

by Daisy Meadows

illustrated by Georgie Ripper

ORCHARD BOOKS

The
Fairyland
Palace

Forest

Sweet Factory

The
Village
Hall

River

Wetherbury Village

Fa

Jack Frost's
Ice Castle

en Wood

Mrs. Fordham's Cottage

The Park

Willow Hill

The Museum

The High St.

sty's
use

Fields

Mudhole

N
←W E→
S

Goblins green and goblins small,
I cast this spell to make you tall.
As high as the palace you shall grow.
My icy magic makes it so.

Then steal Doodle's magic feathers,
Used by the fairies to make all weathers.
Climate chaos I have planned
On Earth, and here, in Fairyland!

Contents

A Sunny Spell

"I feel as if I'm about to melt," said
Rachel Walker happily.

It was a hot summer afternoon and she
and her friend, Kirsty Tate, were enjoying
the sunshine in Kirsty's back garden. A
bumblebee buzzed lazily around Mrs Tate's
sunflowers, and a single breath of wind
whispered through the yellow rose bushes.

The weather had been so warm and sunny, Mr and Mrs Tate had given the girls permission to camp out in the garden that night. Kirsty looked up from a jumble of tent poles and bright orange material she was sorting through. "It's been a perfect day," she agreed. "Let's hope tonight is perfect, too. I don't fancy lying out here in the rain, do you?"

Rachel laughed, and started untangling tent pegs with her friend. "I think I'd rather have a shower in the morning, not in the middle of the night," she agreed.

Kirsty held up some poles. "Right. How do we put this thing together, then?" she asked brightly.

Rachel scratched her head. "Well..." she began.

"Need some help?" came a voice from behind them.

"Dad!" said Kirsty in relief. "Yes, please. We—" She burst out laughing as she looked at her father.

Rachel turned to see what was so funny. She had to bite her lip not to laugh, too. For there, standing in front of them, was Mr Tate, wearing the most enormous sunglasses she had ever seen.

Mr Tate was looking very pleased. He waggled the glasses up and down on his nose. "Do you like my new shades?" he asked.

"Well, yes," Kirsty said, trying to keep a straight face. "They're very... summery."

Mr Tate knelt down and started putting the tent together. "The weather has been strange all week, I didn't know whether to buy them or not," he said. "I hope it doesn't start snowing again!"

Rachel and Kirsty looked at each other but didn't say anything. They shared a very special secret. They knew *exactly* why the weather had been so strange – Jack Frost had been messing it all up.

Doodle, the fairy weather-vane cockerel, usually looked after the weather with his seven magic tail feathers. But Jack Frost had cast a spell to make his goblin servants bigger and sent them to steal Doodle's feathers. Without them, the weather had gone completely haywire. Rachel and Kirsty were helping the Weather Fairies to get them back, but until that time, Doodle was just an ordinary iron weather-vane on top of the Tates' barn.

Yesterday, with the help of Pearl the Cloud Fairy, Kirsty and Rachel had returned the Cloud Feather to Doodle. But there were still four feathers left to find.

"There!" said Mr Tate, stepping back and admiring the finished tent. "It's all yours."

"Thanks, Dad," Kirsty said as he walked away. She put two sleeping bags inside the tent and then flopped down on the grass. "Phew!" she whistled. "It's still so hot! I hope it cools down soon, or we'll never be able to sleep in there." Rachel was frowning and looking at her watch.

"Kirsty," she said slowly. "Have you noticed where the sun is?"

Kirsty looked up and pointed. "Right there, in the sky," she replied helpfully.

"Yes, but look how high it is," Rachel insisted. "It hasn't even *started* setting yet."

Kirsty glanced at her watch. "But it's half-past seven," she said. Now she was frowning, too. "So that can't be right."

Rachel had just opened her mouth to
reply, when suddenly there was a loud
Pop! "What was that?" she whispered.

Pop! Pop! Pop!

"It sounds like it's coming from the
other side of the hedge," Kirsty
answered, her eyes wide. "But there's
only a cornfield over there."

Pop! Pop! Pop!

Curiously, the girls peeped over the hedge to see what was making all the noise. And then they both gasped out loud.

Goldie Drops In

"I don't believe it," Kirsty said, rubbing her eyes. "Is that what I think it is?"

Pop! Pop! Pop!

Rachel nodded. "Popcorn," she breathed.

It was an amazing sight. The sun was so hot that the corn in the field was literally cooking — and turning into popcorn!

Both girls stared as golden puffs of corn
bounced everywhere. It was just
as if the field was one
enormous saucepan.
A delicious smell of
popcorn drifted over
the hedge, and both
girls sniffed hungrily.

Kirsty and Rachel looked
at each other, and grinned.

"There's definitely magic
in the air," Kirsty said.

"It must be the goblin
with the Sunshine Feather,"
Rachel agreed, feeling her
heart beat faster with excitement.

Both girls peered hard at the
field, hoping to spot a goblin lurking
somewhere, but it was difficult to see

clearly through the blizzard of popcorn.
It was still tumbling and twirling
in the sky, like a sandstorm.
Rachel suddenly grabbed
Kirsty's hand.
"Look!" she cried.
Kirsty stared.
Darting above the
corn was a twinkling
yellow light. It was
zigzagging through the air
between the flying pieces of
popcorn and heading straight
towards them. As it came
closer, the air above the field
seemed to glitter with a thousand
tiny sparkles. Both girls could see a
pair of delicate golden wings beating
quickly, and the glimmer of a tiny wand.

"It's Goldie the Sunshine Fairy," whispered Rachel in delight.

They held their breath as the fairy weaved in and out of the bouncing corn, neatly dodging each piece. Then she swooped down to land on the hedge in front of them. "Phew!" she laughed. "Talk about a bumpy ride!"

Kirsty and Rachel
watched as Goldie
shook popcorn dust
from her glittering,
golden-edged
wings. Her face
was framed by
long, curly, blonde
hair, and she wore a
gauzy dress in fiery reds,
yellows and oranges. A tiny gold
tiara glinted in her hair and shiny
red bangles glimmered on her wrists.

"Hello again," said Goldie. "I've
been hearing all about how you've
helped Crystal, Abigail and Pearl.
You've done brilliantly!"

Rachel and Kirsty grinned at
each other proudly.

"The goblin who has the Sunshine Feather can't be far away," Goldie went on, looking up at the sky where the sun was still blazing as brightly as ever.

"That's what we thought," Kirsty said. "There's a farm on the other side of this field. Shall we start looking there?"

"Good idea," Goldie replied cheerfully. But then her face fell as she looked at the cornfield again. Popcorn was still whizzing around like hot white missiles. "Is there another way across the field, though?"

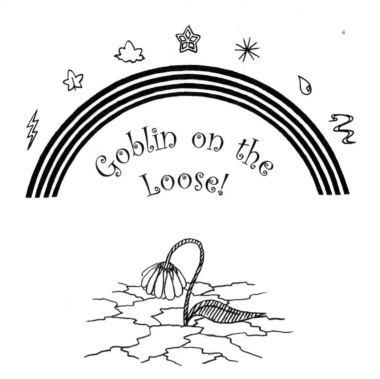

Goblin on the Loose!

Goldie sighed. "I don't fancy dodging that popcorn again," she said. She leaned back to examine a scorch mark on one of her wings. "I almost burned myself last time."

"There's a lane that runs down the side of the field to the farm," Kirsty told her. "We'll ask Mum if we can go for a quick walk before bedtime."

Minutes later, the three of them were on their way. The air was practically shimmering with heat. There were cracks in the ground where the earth had become hardened by the sun, flowers wilted in the hedgerow, and the grass was turning dry and brown. There wasn't even the slightest gasp of wind now. Once they reached the farm, the girls and Goldie started searching for the goblin.

First they peeped into the stables.
Two very hot-looking horses were
sheltering from the sun. "Hello," Goldie
said. "I don't suppose you've seen a
goblin hanging around, have you?"

One of the horses shook her mane.

"All we've seen is this stable," she said.
"And there are no goblins in here."

"It's too hot to go out," the other
horse whinnied.

Next the girls
and Goldie
slipped into the
cowshed. The
cows were all
half-asleep in the
heat, and quite
grumpy at being
disturbed. There was no goblin.

At last the three friends came
to the duck pond. They
wondered if the goblin
might be cooling off in
the water, but there was
no sign of him − or the
Sunshine Feather.

"You should ask the pigs,"
a duck quacked helpfully
from a shady spot in the reeds.

"They've been grumbling all day about something or other. And pigs are nosy. If there's a goblin on the farm, they'll know about it."

Goldie thanked the duck politely. "I think I can hear the pigs over here," Rachel said, leading the way around the side of the farmhouse.

Soon they could all hear the grunting. The duck was right, the pigs seemed very upset about something. They all turned to look curiously at Goldie, though, when she flew over to speak to them.

Goldie fluttered down to perch on the biggest pig's snout. "What's the problem?" she asked kindly.

The pig squinted at the golden fairy in front of his little blue eyes. "It's like this," he began, in a cross, squeaky kind of voice. "It's been so hot that the farmer topped up the mudhole with water, so that us pigs could keep nice and cool." He twitched his ears indignantly. "But someone else has pinched our spot in the mud – and he won't let us in!"

"It's not fair," a piglet squealed, running up to Rachel and Kirsty. "It's not fa-a-a-air!"

"It certainly isn't," Kirsty agreed, giving him a pat.

"It sounds like just the kind of trick a goblin would play!" Rachel pointed out. "Where is the mudhole?"

The pigs gave directions and the girls set off with Goldie flying above their heads. Rachel crossed her fingers. She felt quite sure that they would find a goblin in the mud. Who else would be mean enough to stop the pigs from wallowing in their own mud pool?

They hadn't been walking for very long when they heard someone singing in a croaky, tuneless voice:

*"I've been having so much fun
Blasting out this golden sun.
It's roasting, toasting, popcorn weather.
Oh, how I love my Sunshine Feather!"*

Kirsty, Rachel and Goldie dived behind a nearby tree at once, and carefully peeped out. There, right in the middle of the mudhole, covered in thick, wet mud, was an extremely cheerful goblin. He waved the Sunshine Feather in the air as he sang, and each time it moved, golden sunbeams flooded from its tip, making the air feel even hotter.

When he got to the end of his song, he started all over again, splashing his feet in the mud in time to the words. "I've been having so much fun..."

"What shall we do?" Kirsty whispered. The goblin was holding the feather so tightly, it looked like it would be impossible to take it from him.

Goldie twirled around in frustration.

"I hate seeing him with my Sunshine Feather," she muttered, folding her arms across her chest. "Look, he's got it all muddy!"

Rachel frowned. "Maybe we could distract him somehow, then dash over and grab the feather while he's looking the other way."

"I don't fancy dashing through all that slippery mud," Kirsty said quietly, eyeing it doubtfully. "We'll probably fall over. And look, he's right in the middle of it. He'll be able to spot us coming way before we get there."

They drew further away from the mudhole so that they could discuss their next move without fear of the goblin

overhearing. After a few minutes,
Rachel held up a hand. "Ssshh! What's
that noise?" she hissed in alarm.

A Bamboozled Goblin

Kirsty, Rachel and Goldie held their breath as they listened to the strange new sound. It was a loud, wheezing, rumbling kind of noise, somewhere between a grunt and a hiss. Grumble-sshhh, it went. Grumble-sshhh. Grumble-sshhh...

It was coming from the direction of

the mudhole. Kirsty and Rachel crept back to the tree and peeped out from behind it, wondering what sort of terrifying creature they were going to see.

When Rachel saw what was making the noise, though, she had to clap her hand over her mouth to stop herself laughing out loud. The wheezy rumble was nothing more than the goblin – snoring!

"At least he isn't singing any more," Kirsty laughed.

Goldie fluttered her
wings hopefully when
she saw that the
goblin was asleep,
and she flew a little
closer to the Sunshine
Feather. But her face
fell when she saw just
how tightly the goblin
was clutching the feather to

his chest in his sleep. She flew back to
the girls, shaking her head. "If I try and
pull it out of his grasp, he's sure to
wake up," she told them. "How are we
going to get that feather?"

A smile appeared on Kirsty's face.
"Maybe we could..." she began
thoughtfully. Then she grinned broadly.
"Yes! That could work!" she declared.

Without another word, she began running back towards her house. "Back in a minute," she called over her shoulder.

Rachel and Goldie watched her go. They were both dying to know what Kirsty was up to. Luckily, they didn't have to wait long for her return. And when she came back, she looked quite different!

"What *is* she wearing?" Goldie murmured to Rachel as they saw Kirsty running towards them.

"Her dad's sunglasses," Rachel replied, staring at her friend with great interest. She was starting to wonder if Kirsty had been in the sun for too long. Why had she brought the enormous sunglasses with her? And why was she carrying a fishing rod?

Kirsty grinned at the confused expressions on their faces. "I'll explain everything," she promised, reaching up to rest the fishing rod in the tree. "First, we need to shrink to fairy size, Rachel." Both Kirsty and Rachel had been given beautiful gold lockets by the Fairy Queen. Inside each locket was magical fairy dust. A tiny pinch of the sparkling dust was enough to turn the girls into fairies in the twinkling of an eye!

Kirsty and Rachel sprinkled themselves with fairy dust. It glittered a bright sunshine-yellow in the light and then – whoosh – they were getting smaller and smaller and smaller. The tree next to them became enormous as the girls shrank to the size of Goldie.

Kirsty and Rachel fluttered their wings in delight. They both loved being fairies.

"Now then," Kirsty said. "Fly up to the tree and I'll tell you my plan."

They all perched by the fishing rod, and Goldie and Rachel watched as Kirsty's nimble fingers balanced the sunglasses on the end of the fishing hook.

"We're going to let the fishing line out slowly," Kirsty told them quietly, "and lower the sunglasses onto the goblin's nose."

"Why?" Rachel wanted to know.

"Do you think they'll suit him?" Goldie asked.

Kirsty shook her head, trying not to laugh. "With sunglasses on, everything will look dark to him," she whispered. "With a bit of luck, he'll think the Sunshine Feather has broken!"

Goldie clapped her hands in delight.

"Oh, what a good idea!" she cried. "I do love to play tricks on those mean old goblins."

Very carefully, Kirsty, Rachel and Goldie turned the wheel of the fishing rod and lowered the sunglasses all the way down to the goblin. Kirsty held her breath as the sunglasses landed right on the end of his nose. Perfect!

They reeled in the fishing line and then Goldie waved her wand to release a stream of magical, sunny fairy dust. Little golden sparkles fizzed and popped like firecrackers around the goblin's head until he woke with a start.

He opened his eyes and blinked when he saw that everything seemed to have gone dark. "My feather's broken!" he moaned, giving it a shake. "Shine, you stupid sun!" he commanded.

Of course, the Sunshine Feather wasn't broken at all. As soon as the goblin shook it, the sun shone more brilliantly than ever. But as far as the goblin could see, the world remained in darkness.

He waved the feather again. "I said, shine!" he ordered, in frustration. The sun shone obediently as if it were the middle of the day, but the goblin could see no change. Twice more he shook the feather and twice more the sun shone hotter and brighter, but through the sunglasses, the goblin saw only twilight. As far as he knew, the Sunshine Feather was having no effect. "Broken!" the goblin finally announced crossly, and he threw the feather away in disgust.

Goldie shot out of the tree at once,
like a little golden firework.
While the goblin was
still muttering gloomily
to himself, Goldie
swooped down and
grabbed the feather.
"Thank you!" she
sang happily,
hugging it tightly
as she flew back
to the girls. Kirsty's
plan had worked!

With another
sprinkle of fairy dust,
Rachel and Kirsty turned
themselves human again
and started scrambling down
from the tree with the fishing rod.

The goblin spotted them and jumped to his feet. As he did so, the sunglasses bounced on his nose. "Sunglasses?" he exclaimed, sounding puzzled as he reached up to grab the glasses. He pushed them onto the top of his head and peered at the girls, blinking in the dazzling sunlight. "You tricked me!" he yelled in fury when he saw Goldie clutching the Sunshine Feather. "Come back with that feather!"

Kirsty and Rachel looked at each other fearfully. Now that Jack Frost's goblins were so big, they seemed more scary than ever. And this one looked very angry at having been outwitted.

He shook his fist and ran straight towards the girls.

"Run!" shouted Kirsty.

Happy Pigs

Rachel grabbed Kirsty's hand
and they both ran towards the
farmhouse as fast as they could.
The goblin was right behind them,
making a horrible growling sound
in his throat.

"Give me back that feather! Give
it back!" he screamed angrily.

Rachel's heart thumped painfully in her chest as she ran. The goblin was closing on them. She could hear his breathing, hoarse and ragged. The goblin stretched out his hand to grab her and she gasped as she felt his fingertips brush her shoulder.

"Got y—" he began. Then his voice turned from anger to confusion. "Hey! What's happening?"

With a swirl of dancing sunbeams,
Goldie had waved the Sunshine Feather
and pointed it straight at the goblin. At
once, the sun beat down fiercely upon
him – and the thick mud that
smothered him started drying rapidly.
As his legs became stiff and heavy with
the solidifying mud, the goblin slowed.
Then, as the mud set hard, the goblin
found he couldn't move at all.

"No-o-o-!" he wailed in despair.

Despite having been so scared just a few seconds earlier, the girls found themselves smiling at the sight of the goblin. "He's a goblin statue!" Rachel exclaimed, laughing.

Only his eyes moved now. They flicked back and forth wildly as the goblin glared first at the girls, and then at Goldie who was fluttering beside them. Kirsty noticed her dad's sunglasses on top of the goblin's head. She took a cautious step towards him. And another. The goblin remained motionless, so she marched right up to him and carefully took the glasses.

"I'll have these back now, I think," she said. "If I'd known how useful these sunglasses would be, I'd never have laughed at Dad for wearing them!" she told Rachel.

Goldie and the girls made their way back to the farmhouse where the pigs were waiting expectantly.

"The mudhole is all yours again," Goldie said to the pigs in her sweet silvery voice. "You'll find a new goblin scarecrow nearby," she added. "But don't worry. He won't be in any hurry to go back into the mud."

The pigs grunted joyfully and started trotting off in search of their cool mud pool. The smallest piglet nuzzled around Kirsty and Rachel's legs before he went. "Thank you," he squealed happily.

Rachel watched them go. "What
will happen to the goblin?" she asked.
"He won't have to stay there for ever,
will he?"

Goldie's eyes twinkled mischievously.
"Not for ever, no," she said. "He'll get
out of the mud as soon as it rains." She
smiled cheerfully. "Jack Frost won't be
pleased with him when he finds out
we've got the Sunshine Feather back,
though!"

Now that they were out of danger, Goldie waved the Sunshine Feather with an expert flourish and the sun began to set – just as it was supposed to. The girls watched as the sky was flooded with orange and pink and a rich deep red.

"Let's take the Sunshine Feather back

to Doodle," Kirsty said happily. "And then we'd better go to bed!"

Rachel was yawning. "It's been another busy day, hasn't it?" she smiled.

With the sun setting, the warmth was quickly ebbing away and the girls soon found themselves shivering in their thin T-shirts. Goldie fluttered above them with the Sunshine Feather, tapping it gently to sprinkle a few sunbeams onto their bare arms to keep them warm.

It was almost dark by the time they got back to Kirsty's garden. They could just about see the silhouette of Doodle perched on the barn roof.

Goldie flew up to give the cockerel back his magic feather. As she did so, Doodle came to life, his fiery feathers glowing brilliant colours in the twilight. He turned to look at Rachel and Kirsty. "Will come—" he squawked urgently. But, before he could say any more, the magic drained away, his colours faded and he became a rusty old weather-vane once again.

Each time the girls managed to return one of Doodle's feathers, the cockerel came to life for a few brief moments and squawked a couple of words. Rachel frowned as she pieced together all the words that Doodle had said to them so far. "Beware! Jack Frost will come..." she murmured, feeling an icy shiver down her spine as if Jack Frost was already there. "It's a warning, Kirsty. Let's hope he's not coming soon!"

Goldie looked worried. "Take care, girls. And thank you for everything," she said. She blew them a stream of fairy kisses that sparkled in the darkening sky. "I must go back to Fairyland now. Goodbye!"

Kirsty and Rachel watched Goldie fly away until she was nothing more than a tiny golden speck in the distance. Then, just as they were about to get ready for bed, they heard footsteps and Mr Tate came out of the house. He was looking around, a puzzled expression on his face. "Did I just hear a cockerel crowing?" he asked.

"A cockerel? At this time of day?" Kirsty replied innocently.

Mr Tate frowned. "I must be hearing things," he said, turning to go back inside. "Good night, girls. Sleep well." Then he glanced up at Doodle as he headed back towards the house. "I'm sure that weather-vane had a smaller tail," he muttered, then shook his head. "Seeing things as well! Definitely time to call it a night..."

Kirsty and Rachel smiled at each other. "Only three more feathers to find," Kirsty said. "I wonder which one will be next!"

RAINBOW magic

The Weather Fairies

Crystal, Abigail, Pearl and Goldie
have got their feathers back. Now
Rachel and Kirsty must help

Evie the Mist Fairy

A Misty Morning

"Wake up, sleepy head!" cried Kirsty
Tate to her friend, Rachel, as she jumped
out of bed and started to dress.

Rachel Walker was asleep in the spare
bed in Kirsty's room. She was staying
with Kirsty and her parents in the village
of Wetherbury. Sleepily, she rolled over
and opened her eyes. "I was dreaming

that we were back in Fairyland," she told
Kirsty. "The weather was
topsy-turvy – sunny and snowing all
at the same time – and Doodle was
trying to sort it out." Doodle, the
fairies' magic weather cockerel, had
been on Rachel's mind a lot lately,
because she and Kirsty were on an
important fairy mission!

Each day in Fairyland, with the help
of the Weather Fairies, Doodle used his
magic tail feathers to organise the
weather. Each of the seven magic feathers
controlled a different kind of weather, and
each of the seven Weather Fairies was
responsible for working with one feather
in particular. The system worked perfectly
until mean old Jack Frost sent seven
goblins to steal Doodle's magic feathers.

The goblins ran off into the human world with one feather each, and when poor Doodle followed them out of Fairyland, he found himself transformed into a rusty metal weather-vane. The Queen of the Fairies had asked Rachel and Kirsty to help find the magic feathers and return them to Doodle.

Meanwhile, Fairyland's weather was all mixed up – and the goblins had been using the feathers to cause weather chaos in the human world too.

"Poor Doodle," Kirsty said, looking out of the window at the old barn where the cockerel was perched. Her dad had found Doodle lying in the park, and thinking he was an ordinary weather vane, Mr Tate had brought him home and put him on the barn roof.

"Hopefully we'll find another magic feather today," Kirsty continued. "We've already found four of the stolen feathers. We just need to find the other three and then Doodle will get his magic back."

"Yes," Rachel agreed, brightening at the thought. "But I have to go home in three days, so we don't have long!" As she gazed out at the blue sky, a wisp of silvery mist caught her eye. "Look, that cloud is shaped just like a feather!" she said.

Win a Rainbow Magic
Sparkly T-Shirt and Goody Bag!

In every book in the Rainbow Magic Weather series
(books 8-14) there is a hidden picture of a magic
feather with a secret letter in it. Find all seven letters
and re-arrange them to make a special Fairyland
word, then send it to us. Each month we will put
the entries into a draw. The winner will receive a
Rainbow Magic Sparkly T-shirt and Goody Bag!

Send your entry on a postcard to Rainbow Magic
Competition, Orchard Books, 96 Leonard Street,
London EC2A 4XD. Australian readers should write
to 32/45-51 Huntley Street, Alexandria, NSW 2015.
Don't forget to include your name and address.

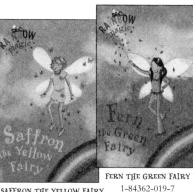

FERN THE GREEN FAIRY
1-84362-019-7

SAFFRON THE YELLOW FAIRY
1-84362-018-9

AMBER THE ORANGE FAIRY
1-84362-017-0

RUBY THE RED FAIRY
1-84362-016-2

HEATHER THE VIOLET FAIRY
1-84362-022-7

IZZY THE INDIGO FAIRY
1-84362-021-9

SKY THE BLUE FAIRY
1-84362-020-0

RAINBOW magic

The Weather Fairies

CRYSTAL THE SNOW FAIRY
1-84362-633-0

ABIGAIL THE BREEZE FAIRY
1-84362-634-9

PEARL THE CLOUD FAIRY
1-84362-635-7

GOLDIE THE SUNSHINE FAIRY
1-84362-641-1

EVIE THE MIST FAIRY
1-84362-636-5

STORM THE LIGHTNING FAIRY
1-84362-637-3

HAYLEY THE RAIN FAIRY
1-84362-638-1

Collect all of the Rainbow Magic books!

RAINBOW magic

by Daisy Meadows

The Weather Fairies

✳ ✳ ✳

All priced at £3.99
Rainbow Magic books are available from all good bookshops,
or can be ordered direct from the publisher:
Orchard Books, PO BOX 29, Douglas IM99 1BQ
Credit card orders please telephone 01624 836000
or fax 01624 837033 or visit our Internet site: www.wattspub.co.uk
or e-mail: bookshop@enterprise.net for details.

To order please quote title, author and ISBN
and your full name and address.
Cheques and postal orders should be made payable to 'Bookpost plc.'
Postage and packing is FREE within the UK
(overseas customers should add £1.00 per book).

Prices and availability are subject to change.